MYSTERY

Essential Literary Genres

BY REBECCA MORRIS

Essential Library

An Imprint of Abdo Publishing | abdopublishing.com

ABDOPUBLISHING.COM

Published by Abdo Publishing, a division of ABDO, PO Box 398166, Minneapolis, Minnesota 55439. Copyright © 2017 by Abdo Consulting Group, Inc. International copyrights reserved in all countries. No part of this book may be reproduced in any form without written permission from the publisher. Essential Library™ is a trademark and logo of Abdo Publishing.

Printed in the United States of America, North Mankato, Minnesota
102016
012017

Interior Photos: PBS/Photofest, 11; ITV/REX/Shutterstock/Rex USA, 14, 16, 21; PA Wire URN:23718838/Press Association/AP Images, 22–23; John Beard/The Denver Post/ Getty Images, 33; Hallmark Entertainment/Everett Collection, 35, 42; Greg Hall Feature Photo Service/Newscom, 45; Bain News Service/Library of Congress, 54–55; 20th Century Fox/Photofest, 60, 62; Anton Balazh/Shutterstock Images, 65; Abi Warner/Shutterstock Images, 67; Albert Cooper Mirrorpix/Newscom, 71; Scott Adamson, 82–83; Shutterstock Images, 85; MOAimage/Shutterstock Images, 88; THE AGENCY: A SPY IN THE HOUSE. Copyright © 2009 by Y.S. Lee. Reproduced by permission of the publisher, Candlewick Press, Somerville, MA on behalf of Walker Books, London., 91; North Wind Picture Archives, 92–93

Editor: Jenna Gleisner
Series Designer: Maggie Villaume

PUBLISHER'S CATALOGING-IN-PUBLICATION DATA

Names: Morris, Rebecca, author.
Title: Mystery / by Rebecca Morris.
Description: Minneapolis, MN : Abdo Publishing, 2017. | Series: Essential
   literary genres | Includes bibliographical references and index.
Identifiers: LCCN 2016945210 | ISBN 9781680783803 (lib. bdg.) |
   ISBN 9781680797336 (ebook)
Subjects: LCSH: Literature--Juvenile literature. | Literary form--Juvenile
   literature.
Classification: DDC 809--dc23
LC record available at http://lccn.loc.gov/2016945210

CONTENTS

INTRODUCTION TO
LITERARY GENRES

Why do we read and write literature? Telling stories is an integral part of being human, a universal experience across history and cultures. Literature as we know it today is the written form of these stories and ideas. Writing allows authors to take their readers on a journey that crosses the boundaries of space and time. Literature allows us to understand the experiences of others and express experiences of our own.

What Is a Genre?

A genre is a specific category, or type, of literature. Broad genres of literature include nonfiction, poetry, drama, and fiction. Smaller groupings include subject-based genres such as mystery, science fiction, romance, or fantasy. Literature can also be classified by its audience, such as young adult (YA) or children's, or its format, such as a graphic novel or picture book.

What Are Literary Theory and Criticism?

Literary theory gives us tools to help decode a text. On one level, we can examine the words and phrases the author uses so we can interpret or debate his or her message. We can ask questions about how the book's structure creates an effect on the reader, and whether this is the effect the author intended. We can analyze symbolism or themes in a work. We can dive deeper by asking how a work either supports or challenges society and its values or traditions.

You can look at these questions using different criticisms, or schools of thought. Each type of criticism asks you to look at the work from a different perspective. Perhaps you want to examine what the work says about the writer's life or the time period in which the work was created. Biographical or historical criticism considers these questions. Or perhaps you are interested in what the work says about the role of women or the structure of society. Feminist or Marxist theories seek to answer those types of questions.

How Do You Apply Literary Criticism?

You write an analysis when you use a literary or critical approach to examine and question a work. The theory you choose is a lens through which you can view the work, or a springboard for asking questions about the work. Applying a theory helps you think critically. You are free to question the work and make an assertion about it. If you choose to examine a work using racial criticism, for example, you may ask questions about how the work challenges or upholds racial structures in society. Or you may ask how a character's race affects his or her identity or development throughout the work.

Forming a Thesis

Form your questions and find answers in the work or other related materials. Then you can create a thesis. The thesis is the key point in your analysis. It is your argument about the work based on the school of thought you are using. For example, if you want to approach a work using feminist criticism, you could write the following thesis: The character of Margy in Sissy Johnson's *Margy Sings the Blues* uses her songwriting to subvert traditional gender roles.

HOW TO MAKE A THESIS STATEMENT

In an analysis, a thesis statement typically appears at the end of the introductory paragraph. It is usually only one sentence long and states the author's main idea.

Providing Evidence

Once you have formed a thesis, you must provide evidence to support it. Evidence will usually take the form of examples and quotations from the work itself, often including dialogue from a character. You may wish to address what others have written about the work. Quotes from these individuals may help support your claim. If you find any quotes or examples that contradict your thesis, you will need to create an argument against them. For instance: Many critics claim Margy's actions uphold traditional gender roles, even if her songs went against them. However, the novel's resolution proves Margy had the power to change society through her music.

HOW TO SUPPORT A THESIS STATEMENT

An analysis should include several arguments that support the thesis's claim. An argument is one or two sentences long and is supported by evidence from the work being discussed. Organize the arguments into paragraphs. These paragraphs make up the body of the analysis.

Concluding the Essay

After you have written several arguments and included evidence to support them, finish the essay with a conclusion. The conclusion restates the ideas from the

HOW TO CONCLUDE AN ESSAY

Begin your conclusion with a recap of the thesis and a brief summary of the most important or strongest arguments. Leave readers with a final thought that puts the essay in a larger context or considers its wider implications.

thesis and summarizes some of the main points from the essay. The conclusion's final thought often considers additional implications for the essay or gives the reader something to ponder further.

In This Book

In this book, you will read summaries of works, each followed by an analysis. Critical thinking sections will give you a chance to consider other theses and questions about the work. Did you agree with the author's analysis? What other questions are raised by the thesis and its arguments? You can also see other directions the author could have pursued to analyze the work. Then, in the Analyze It section in the final pages of this book, you will have an opportunity to create your own analysis paper.

Mystery

The book you are reading focuses on the essential elements of the mystery genre. The mystery genre is a wide category that has many subgenres within it, but some common elements define a work of fiction as a mystery. In mysteries, there is an unknown driving the plot, the gradual reveal of information, and a conclusion that resolves the unknown. For example, a crime is committed, a detective-type character investigates, and the perpetrator of the crime is exposed. The nature of the unknown component may vary widely, and mysteries may be written in a broad range of tones and styles for several kinds of audiences. However, as long as a work follows the pattern of unknown, gradual reveal of clues, and resolution, we may classify it as a mystery.

LOOK FOR THE GUIDES

Throughout the chapters that analyze the works, thesis statements have been highlighted. The box next to the thesis helps explain what questions are being raised about the work. Supporting arguments have also been highlighted. The boxes next to the arguments help explain how these points support the thesis. The conclusions are also accompanied by explanatory boxes. Look for these guides throughout each analysis.

2

AN OVERVIEW OF
THE MURDER OF ROGER ACKROYD

The Murder of Roger Ackroyd was published by best-selling mystery author Agatha Christie in 1926. *The Murder of Roger Ackroyd,* which features the famous detective Hercule Poirot, was popular at the time of its release, and it continues to receive attention because of its surprise ending.

Death in King's Abbot

The death of Mrs. Ferrars, a wealthy widow, sets off a series of mysterious events in the small village of King's Abbot, England. Dr. James Sheppard tells his sister Caroline that Mrs. Ferrars died of an accidental overdose of sleeping medication. However, Caroline suspects the death to be a suicide, provoked by a guilty conscience,

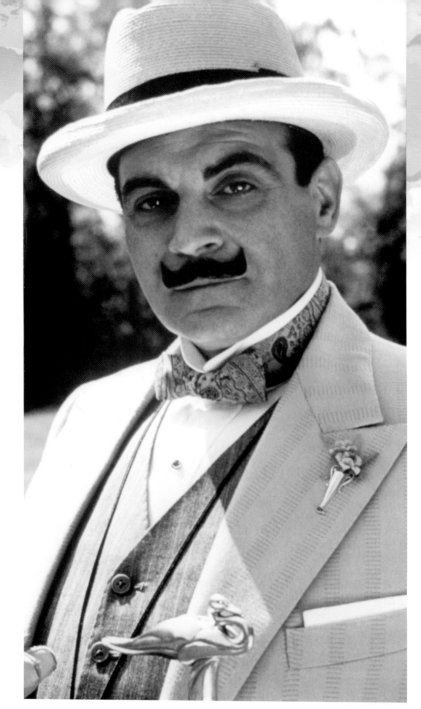

The character Hercule Poirot appears in 33 of Christie's novels, as well as more than 50 of her short stories.

Character	Role
Dr. James Sheppard	narrator and community doctor
Hercule Poirot	private detective and Dr. Sheppard's neighbor
Roger Ackroyd	wealthy widower
Mrs. Ferrars	wealthy widow and Roger Ackroyd's secret fiancé
Ralph Paton	Roger Ackroyd's adopted stepson
Mrs. Cecil Ackroyd	Roger Ackroyd's sister-in-law, the wife of his deceased brother
Flora Ackroyd	Mrs. Ackroyd's daughter, Roger Ackroyd's niece
Miss Russell	Roger Ackroyd's housekeeper
Major Hector Blunt	Roger Ackroyd's friend and houseguest
Geoffrey Raymond	Roger Ackroyd's secretary
Ursula Bourne	maid at Fernly Park, secretly married to Ralph
Charles Kent	Miss Russell's illegitimate son
Inspector Raglan	lead police investigator
Parker	Roger Ackroyd's butler
Caroline Sheppard	Dr. Sheppard's sister
Mr. Hammond	Roger Ackroyd's lawyer

The Murder of Roger Ackroyd character list

as Caroline believes Mrs. Ferrars poisoned her husband a year earlier. She also thinks there was a secret engagement between Mrs. Ferrars and Roger Ackroyd.

As rumors swirl about Mrs. Ferrars's death, other peculiar events occur. Ackroyd's housekeeper, Miss Russell, goes to see Dr. Sheppard about a bad knee, but she also asks him about poisons and drugs. Ralph Paton, Ackroyd's stepson, makes a covert visit to the village, and Caroline overhears him talking to a mystery woman in the woods about inheritance troubles. Finally, Dr. Sheppard's strange new neighbor confirms another secret engagement—this one between Ralph and Ralph's cousin Flora.

The evening after Mrs. Ferrars's death, Ackroyd has Dr. Sheppard over for dinner at his home, Fernly Park. After, Ackroyd takes Dr. Sheppard into his study for a serious talk. Ackroyd alludes to problems with Ralph but does not explain. Then, he confides that he had, in fact, secretly been engaged to Mrs. Ferrars. He also knows she poisoned her husband and that someone had been blackmailing her.

In the evening mail, Ackroyd finds one final letter from Mrs. Ferrars. It identifies the blackmailer, but Ackroyd sends Dr. Sheppard away before he reads it. On his way home, Dr. Sheppard passes a disguised stranger who asks for directions to Fernly Park. Back home with Caroline later that evening, Dr. Sheppard receives a phone call. He tells Caroline the call is from Ackroyd's butler, Parker, with news of Ackroyd's murder.

Dr. Sheppard returns to Fernly Park only to find Parker denying he called. He believes Ackroyd is still in the study, alive and well. Parker and Dr. Sheppard force their way into the study to find that Ackroyd has, in fact, been stabbed to death. The letter from Mrs. Ferrars is missing, and there are footprints outside the window.

Ackroyd, *above*, trusts Dr. Sheppard, inviting him into his home and confiding in him.

The Investigation Begins

The day after Ackroyd's murder, Flora shows up at Dr. Sheppard's, requesting he go with her to speak to his neighbor, Hercule Poirot, a renowned private detective. Flora wants Poirot to investigate her uncle's murder and clear Ralph's name from any suspicion. Meanwhile, Ralph has gone missing.

Dr. Sheppard, Poirot, and the local investigators all go to Fernly Park. Poirot examines the study, asking detailed questions about the scene. While there, one of the investigators lets them know that the call to

Dr. Sheppard about the murder came from a phone booth at King's Abbot Station, not from Fernly Park. Inspector Raglan suspects Ralph based on the footprints and his timetable of people's whereabouts throughout the evening. Poirot and Dr. Sheppard then continue their search for clues, walking to the summerhouse, which is located on the grounds of the main house.

Back at the house, Mr. Hammond, a lawyer, lays out Ackroyd's will. Most of the large fortune goes to Ralph, 20,000 pounds go to Flora, income on some business shares are willed to Mrs. Ackroyd, and smaller sums go to Miss Russell, Raymond, and the cook. While on the topic of money, Raymond adds that Ackroyd had stowed 100 pounds in his room the day of his murder. However, the group finds only 60 pounds when they check. Raglan and Poirot question two maids about the missing sum. Poirot takes special interest in one of the maids, Ursula Bourne, because she was encouraged to quit the day of Ackroyd's murder, presumably for snooping through papers on his desk.

Poirot sends Dr. Sheppard to speak with Ursula's previous employer, who is suspiciously reluctant to answer questions about her. When Dr. Sheppard returns home, he finds Poirot had stopped by to visit

According to Raglan's schedule, Ursula, *right,* has no verified alibi, placing her on Poirot's radar.

Caroline. The two had discussed the case, including the conversation Caroline overheard in the woods and Miss Russell's appointment the morning of Mrs. Ferrars's death. Dr. Sheppard is mad at Caroline for sharing those details because he thinks they make the case against Ralph look bad. Up until this point, he had concealed those details from Poirot. Later that evening, Poirot has Dr. Sheppard over to confront him about withholding facts relevant to the case.

Secrets Are Revealed

By this point in the novel, Poirot has accused all of the characters connected to Ackroyd of hiding something.

Mrs. Ackroyd summons Dr. Sheppard to Fernly Park to confide what she has been hiding. On the day of the murder, she, not Ursula, had been messing with the papers on Ackroyd's desk, looking for his will. On his way out, Dr. Sheppard bumps into Ursula, who asks about news of Ralph and the time of death.

Dr. Sheppard tells Poirot about his conversations with Mrs. Ackroyd and Ursula and more about his appointment with Miss Russell. Poirot is intrigued to hear Miss Russell asked about drugs. While Dr. Sheppard is with Poirot, Raymond arrives to explain what he has been hiding—a bad debt conveniently resolved with the legacy from Ackroyd's will. Poirot points out that many characters stood to profit from Ackroyd's death.

The following morning, a joint funeral is held for Ackroyd and Mrs. Ferrars, after which Poirot and Dr. Sheppard speak with Parker to uncover what he has been hiding. Parker admits to blackmailing his previous master and to eavesdropping on Ackroyd the night of his murder. However, upon questioning him further, reviewing his bankbook, and speaking to Hammond, Poirot thinks it is unlikely that Parker was Ackroyd's blackmailer, and he does not suspect him of being the murderer either.

After lunch, Dr. Sheppard receives a call about a man named Charles Kent, who has been detained. Authorities believe he is the stranger who asked for directions to Fernly Park the night of the murder. Raglan and Poirot go with Dr. Sheppard to identify him. Kent says he was at Fernly Park to visit someone, though he doesn't say who. Kent has a verifiable alibi for the time of the murder.

The next day, Poirot confronts Flora about her lies. Poirot accuses Flora of stealing cash from Ackroyd's bedroom during a window of time when she claimed to be with her uncle. Flora says the allegations are true and that she stuck to her lie to protect Ralph. Blunt then sticks up for Flora. Poirot can see Flora and Blunt are in love and that Flora has stayed by Ralph's side out of loyalty only, not love.

Later that day, Poirot invites Miss Russell to Dr. Sheppard's to discuss Kent, who is in reality her long lost son, returned to England from Canada, seeking money and nursing a bad drug habit. Miss Russell admits meeting Kent in the summerhouse the day of the murder. When she asked Dr. Sheppard about poison and drugs, she was actually seeking information to help her son.

In a few final maneuvers to put the case in order, Poirot runs a false story in the paper about Ralph's arrest, and he arranges to have everyone involved in the case over to his house. After seeing the newspaper story, a very upset Ursula seeks out Poirot. He greets her as Ursula Paton, and she admits her secret marriage to Ralph. The two had quickly fallen in love and married, but they kept it quiet while Ralph tried to pay his debts and find a job. Before any of that could happen, Ackroyd arranged for Ralph and Flora's engagement. They were not in love, but each of them treated it as a business arrangement.

After news of the engagement spread, Ursula and Ralph met twice, once in the woods and once at the summerhouse. In between those meetings, Ursula told Ackroyd about their marriage, and he was furious. Poirot assures Ursula that Ralph has not really been arrested, despite the newspaper story. Dr. Sheppard then leaves to meet a patient. Meanwhile, Poirot looks over the manuscript Dr. Sheppard has been writing to record the case.

The Case Is Closed

When the guests from Fernly Park arrive at Poirot's, he introduces Ursula as Mrs. Paton, and he also brings out Miss Russell and Parker. He then begins to unfold the case. He explains the two meetings in the summerhouse the evening of the murder—one between Miss Russell and Kent, the other between Ursula and Ralph. Based on that information, it would have been impossible for Kent or Ralph to be with Ackroyd at the time of his death.

Then, to everyone's surprise, Ralph enters. It turns out Dr. Sheppard knew where Ralph was all along. He recommended Ralph hide away in a nursing home, posing as an invalid. Ralph had told Dr. Sheppard of his secret marriage and financial troubles, and so after the murder, Dr. Sheppard suggested the ruse because suspicion was sure to fall on Ralph. After that explanation, Poirot announces he knows the murderer is sitting amongst them, and he warns that he will go to Raglan in the morning with the truth.

As the party leaves for the night, Poirot gestures for Dr. Sheppard to remain behind. Poirot runs through some of the more confounding elements of the case one more time and arrives at his conclusion. Dr. Sheppard

Christie waits until the very end of the novel for Poirot to reveal the murderer.

is the murderer and the blackmailer. Being a doctor, Sheppard knew Mrs. Ferrars had poisoned her husband. He used that knowledge to exploit her for money until she finally committed suicide as an escape. Dr. Sheppard knew Mrs. Ferrars would send Ackroyd a suicide letter to explain she took drastic measures because she felt trapped by her blackmailer. As a result, Dr. Sheppard plotted Ackroyd's murder. Poirot leaves Dr. Sheppard to finish his manuscript. Dr. Sheppard does so and then kills himself by overdosing.

3

THE UNRELIABLE NARRATOR

When thinking about what builds the suspense and surprise in mystery fiction, it can be helpful to look at the narrator's point of view and character. The narrator is particularly important in mysteries because he or she often provides access to the clues. In *The Murder of Roger Ackroyd*, Agatha Christie uses an unreliable narrator, which literary critics define as a narrator who lies, deceives, or withholds information. Christie's use of the unreliable narrator not only provides a big twist, but it also emphasizes that, to solve the mystery,

Christie created the character of Dr. Sheppard as an unreliable narrator to create suspense and mystery.

readers must pay attention to the ways in which the narrator presents information and the details that may undermine the narrator's authority.

In *The Murder of Roger Ackroyd*, Christie builds suspense by layering secrets in many of the characters' lives. The biggest shock comes from the revelation that the well-known and supposedly well-meaning narrator, Dr. James Sheppard, is actually the murderer. Through the technique of first-person narration, Christie demonstrates how easily mystery fiction can blur the line between good and evil to create surprise and suspense.

Christie establishes a trusting relationship between the narrator and the readers by structuring the novel as a manuscript written by

THESIS STATEMENT

The introduction concludes with the thesis statement: "Through the technique of first-person narration, Christie demonstrates how easily mystery fiction can blur the line between good and evil to create surprise and suspense." This essay examines how Christie constructs a character who seems good through his narration but who is actually evil.

ARGUMENT ONE

In the first argument, the author contends that the use of the first-person narration builds a connection between the character and the readers: "Christie establishes a trusting relationship between the narrator and the readers by structuring the novel as a manuscript written by Dr. Sheppard."

Dr. Sheppard. Through this technique, Dr. Sheppard presents thoughts, observations, and actions in his own words. Readers are connected to Dr. Sheppard because they share his point of view. Readers feel as if they know Sheppard well because the manuscript provides minor details about his life and attitude. For example, Sheppard tells readers he "detest[s]" Irish whiskey, and he makes the humorous assumption that his new neighbor, Hercule Poirot, is a hairdresser.[1] This sharing of opinions establishes a close bond between the readers and Dr. Sheppard.

Readers may think they can trust Dr. Sheppard as a narrator and good man because he is a well-respected doctor, confidant, and brother. Dr. Sheppard is well-known as the small community's doctor. Throughout the novel, he often mentions going on his rounds to see patients. He also treats several characters. Sheppard's attention to his patients

ARGUMENT TWO

In the second argument, the author continues exploring the relationship between the readers and the narrator. This argument looks at how the narrator's strong character encourages readers to see him as good: "Readers may think they can trust Dr. Sheppard as a narrator and good man because he is a well-respected doctor, confidant, and brother."

and his acquaintances portray him as a trustworthy and hardworking professional.

Many authoritative characters do, in fact, trust Dr. Sheppard with important information and secrets. Before his murder, Ackroyd talks to Dr. Sheppard about his secret engagement to Mrs. Ferrars and the trouble she was in with the killing of her husband and the blackmail. Poirot sends Dr. Sheppard on errands related to the case and discusses details with him. Other characters confide in Dr. Sheppard as well. Because others place the important secrets of their lives in his hands, Dr. Sheppard appears to be a good and honest ally.

Finally, Dr. Sheppard's character is built up through his relationship with his sister Caroline. The two live together, and Dr. Sheppard provides for Caroline financially. Dr. Sheppard makes no secret that he views Caroline as a meddlesome gossip, and she in turn views him as a "precious old humbug."[2] However, the pestering and small annoyances seem to be the normal kind found in any sibling relationship. Dr. Sheppard also points out Caroline's strengths, noting "there is a lot of kindness in Caroline."[3] This generous attitude toward Caroline and his domestic relationship with her also portray him as a reliable character.

The first-person format and Dr. Sheppard's trustworthiness equip him with the tools to commit evil. Small hints Dr. Sheppard could be misusing his confidences and his manuscript build suspense. At times, he fails to tell Poirot some of the relevant facts and secrets others share with him. For example, he does not reveal his visit with Miss Russell, during which she asked him about drugs and poison. He also does not tell Poirot that Caroline overheard Ralph talking to a mystery woman in the woods the day of his stepfather's murder. At other times, Dr. Sheppard includes comments that may make readers second-guess his truthfulness. For instance, he once remarks, "Fortunately words, ingeniously used, will serve to mask the ugliness of naked facts."[4] This comment suggests Dr. Sheppard knows how to use words to hide unpleasant, even evil, truths.

ARGUMENT THREE

For the third argument, the author shows how Dr. Sheppard manipulates the first-person narrative and strong character for his evil purposes: "The first-person format and Dr. Sheppard's trustworthiness equip him with the tools to commit evil."

The suspense leads up to the surprising climax in which Dr. Sheppard is identified as the murderer. Readers discover he has blackmailed Mrs. Ferrars and murdered Roger Ackroyd. Furthermore, readers discover Dr. Sheppard has exploited his sister's trust, using her as a witness to the phone call from Parker reporting Ackroyd's murder. In actuality, that phone call did not come from Parker. It was a staged call placed to go through when Dr. Sheppard knew Caroline would be there to witness it.

Through Dr. Sheppard's character, Christie shows good and evil are not always easy to discern in a mystery. The attributes that make Dr. Sheppard appear trustworthy are his first-person narration and his roles as doctor, confidant, and brother. However, those are the very same attributes that allow him to commit the crime. Christie uses the shock value of an unreliable narrator to create surprise in her mystery.

CONCLUSION

The final paragraph is the conclusion, which restates the thesis and summarizes the argument. The conclusion reiterates the use of first-person narrative technique and summarizes Dr. Sheppard's good and bad qualities. The conclusion emphasizes that the blurring of good and bad through first-person narrative technique is a prominent feature of the mystery genre that is still relevant today.

THINKING
CRITICALLY

Now it is your turn to assess the essay. Consider these questions:

1. Do you agree with the author's thesis? Is there any evidence in *The Murder of Roger Ackroyd* that disproves this theory?

2. Which of the essay's three arguments do you believe is the most persuasive? What makes that argument more persuasive than the other two?

3. What is another argument you could add to support the author's thesis?

OTHER

APPROACHES

Christie wrote *The Murder of Roger Ackroyd* in the golden age of detective fiction of the 1920s and 1930s. In addition to the now-popular unreliable narrator, other key features and trends such as the use of red herrings and the locked-room mystery were coming into the spotlight. Other approaches might focus on those features or trends.

Red Herrings in Mystery Fiction

Throughout *The Murder of Roger Ackroyd*, several characters act as red herrings. In mystery fiction, red herrings are characters, story lines, or details created as a distraction or diversion to throw the reader off track. A thesis statement for this argument could be: By presenting so many secretive characters as red herrings, Christie implies that fallibility is a normal part of human nature and that it is natural to want to hide one's faults.

Agatha Christie and the Locked-Room Mystery

The locked-room mystery is when a crime, usually a murder, takes place in a confined space. It often seems as if a crime would be unlikely in the area because only a limited number of people have access to it. Some literary scholars find the locked-room mystery appealing because it shows chaos and evil can be controlled. A thesis statement for this argument could be: In *The Murder of Roger Ackroyd*, Christie puts a spin on the locked-room mystery by showing that both crime and detection can be ordered, logical processes.

AN OVERVIEW OF

THE WESTING GAME

Ellen Raskin's *The Westing Game* was published in 1978. The novel has received praise for being a witty, multilayered, and engaging mystery that embraces diversity of many kinds. It won the Newbery Medal, a prestigious prize for children's literature.

Mystery at Sunset Towers

The Westing Game opens on the Fourth of July, presumably in the 1970s when the book was written and published. Otis Amber, a 62-year-old delivery person, distributes letters from property manager Barney Northrup to people mysteriously chosen to live in the new Sunset Towers apartment building. The people come from a diverse range of ages and backgrounds,

Raskin, *right*, who was a children's writer and illustrator, talks about the value of children's books with her husband, *left*, in 1971.

but they all struggle in their own ways, whether with finances, confidence, loneliness, or some other problem.

Sunset Towers overlooks Westing House, which has not been occupied for 15 years. Westing House was once the residence of business tycoon Sam Westing, a self-made man who built a lucrative life after growing up as the orphan son of humble immigrants. He is the epitome of the American Dream. Some say Westing abandoned the home to move to a private island. Others say he died and his body is still in the house. One day at the end of October, the Sunset Towers residents notice smoke coming from Westing House's chimney.

On Halloween, 13-year-old Turtle Wexler goes into Westing House on a bet, where she sees Sam Westing's body tucked into bed. It appears waxy and fresh. She tells no one except for Doug Hoo, another teenage resident of Sunset Towers, but the next morning, there is a newspaper heading that reads "Sam Westing Found Dead." The article mentions the high points of Westing's life, but it also mentions some troubles. These include the death of his daughter Violet just before her wedding, the disappearance of his troubled ex-wife, a lawsuit over the rights to a paper diaper that an inventor says Westing stole and manufactured without permission,

Turtle Wexler, played by Ashley Peldon, *left*, is the mystery's youngest and arguably most clever character.

a car accident on the way to trial, and Westing's disappearance right after that accident.

The Game Rules

That same day, Otis delivers 16 letters from Attorney E. J. Plum, asking recipients to attend the reading of Westing's will. Fifteen of the letters are addressed to characters who either live in or are connected to Sunset Towers, and the sixteenth is addressed to Otis himself. In the will, Westing calls those 16 people his heirs, while identifying himself as "Uncle Sam." He further writes that one amongst them has taken his life. He charges the group with the task of uncovering the guilty person. He calls this task the Westing Game. The heirs are paired up: Madame Hoo and Jake Wexler, Turtle and Flora Baumbach, Chris Theodorakis and Denton Deere, Sandy McSouthers and Judge J. J. Ford, Grace Wexler and James Hoo, Berthe Erica Crow and Otis, Theo Theodorakis and Doug, Sydelle Pulaski and Angela Wexler. Each pair receives a different set of clues and a check for $10,000. The pair that wins will inherit the $200 million estate.

The clues appear to be random words such as *For Plain Grain Shed* and *Sea Mountain Am O*, and most of the heirs are confused. The rules explain that the clues are not supposed to make sense right away. The rules also state that heirs should pay attention to what seems to be missing from the clues, and they instruct heirs to be on the lookout for people lying about their identities.

The Game Begins

The next day, a snowstorm strikes, which traps most of the heirs in Sunset Towers. The next evening, Judge Ford invites all residents to a party at her apartment. Just before the party begins, she receives a phone call from a newspaper reporter, whom she has hired to research the heirs. The judge does not believe Westing was murdered. Instead, she thinks he has designed an elaborate ploy to get revenge on one of the heirs.

The following morning, the heirs meet in the Theodorakis's coffee shop to discuss the will and the clues, but an explosion interrupts the meeting. Back upstairs, the newspaper reporter calls Judge Ford again. He has found pictures from a party hosted 20 years earlier, one of which shows Violet Westing with her escort, George Theodorakis. The judge now knows there are several people connected to Westing— Mr. Hoo (who sued Westing over the paper diaper rights), Chris and Theo through their father (Violet's escort at the party), Sandy (who was fired from Westing paper mill), and herself (later revealed that her mother was the Westings' maid). Judge Ford decides she needs to hire a detective to find out more.

That night, many of the heirs dine at Mr. Hoo's restaurant. Mrs. Wexler (Mr. Hoo's partner in the game), who has started working as the restaurant's hostess, seats people in new pairings, which leads to new information. For example, Mrs. Baumbach tells Judge Ford that Angela reminds her of Violet Westing. While everyone is still in the restaurant, there is another explosion. Sydelle Pulaski is taken to the hospital with a fractured ankle, accompanied by her partner Angela.

With the roads finally cleared from the snowstorm, residents of Sunset Towers start to make their way out of the building and carry on with their lives and the game. Meanwhile, Theo discovers the origin to a line from the will that the heirs have been wondering about: "May God thy gold refine." It's the third verse from "America the Beautiful."

Later, Sandy and Judge Ford meet in her apartment to exchange more details, focusing especially on heirs who may have known Mrs. Westing. They take another look at the photograph of Violet Westing and George Theodorakis and discuss the rumor that Violet had killed herself because she really wanted to marry George instead of the politician she was engaged to. Sandy and the judge also agree Angela looks a lot like Violet.

Meanwhile, at Angela's wedding shower, there is another explosion, injuring Angela. She is taken to share a hospital room with Pulaski. Both Turtle and Pulaski figure out Angela constructed the explosives as a way of releasing her frustrations. She is upset people recognize her only for her beautiful looks and not for her mind or personality.

Friendships and Hidden Connections

As the heirs continue working on their theories, many of them grow closer to their partners: Denton finds promising medical possibilities for wheelchair-bound Chris, and Mr. Wexler teaches Madame Hoo some English. Pairs make headway on their clues as well, but the team that makes the clearest progress is Judge Ford and Sandy, who continue gathering biographical details about the heirs and their connections to one another and to Sam Westing. They discover some particularly interesting information about Crow. For example, her ex-husband's name is Windy Windkloppel. *Windkloppel* also happens to be Mrs. Wexler's real maiden name, though she tells people her maiden name is Windsor. What's more, Crow seems especially attached to Angela, whom she refers to as "that beautiful, innocent angel reborn."[1]

Judge Ford and Sandy also talk to George Theodorakis. He tells them about his relationship with Violet Westing, which was ended by Mrs. Westing because she wanted Violet to marry someone important. Heartbroken and frustrated, Violet committed suicide. Judge Ford and Sandy believe Sam Westing has arranged the game to punish the person who hurt him the most—his ex-wife. Judge Ford further believes the former Mrs. Westing is among the heirs, not actually missing, and that she needs protection.

Meanwhile, Turtle tells everyone she is the bomber to protect Angela. The police hand her over to Judge Ford rather than arresting her. Even though Judge Ford knows Turtle is covering for Angela, she lets both girls get away with it. In their meeting, Turtle also tells the judge about the night she entered the Westing House. When asked why she did not report the murder, Turtle explains she did not think Westing had been murdered because he looked like a sleeping wax dummy. That piques the judge's interest, and Turtle wonders if the body really was a wax dummy instead of a corpse.

At the hospital, Angela and Pulaski figure out the clues spell out almost all of the song "America the Beautiful." Back at the apartments, Judge Ford finishes piecing together the biographical information. She thinks Crow must be Mrs. Westing. Crow herself also begins to worry that Sam Westing has arranged the game to get revenge on Violet's killer. She tells Otis she thinks she is in danger.

The End of the Game

On Saturday night, the heirs assemble at Westing House, following instructions from Attorney Plum. Each of the pairs gives the answer they have arrived at based on the clues. Attorney Plum reads a document, stating that all the answers are wrong and that the guilty is still among them. The heirs then put their clues together to match the song "America the Beautiful." They realize a few words and letters are missing. The missing words and letters spell out "Berthe Erica Crow." At that point, Judge Ford realizes Crow is, in fact, the former Mrs. Westing and Sandy is actually Sam Westing. Before she can do anything about it, Sandy collapses.

Sandy is pronounced dead. Attorney Plum then reads another document, which explains that Sam Westing was born Sam "Windy" Windkloppel. He changed his name for business. The document also explains that no one will win the inheritance if no correct answer is given. The heirs all know the answer is Berthe Erica Crow, but no one turns Crow in, even with the prospect of missing out on millions. Finally, Crow admits her name is the answer. She is then arrested.

However, Turtle realizes there are still parts of the mystery that have not been resolved, so she stages a trial.

After the heirs share their answers, it is revealed to readers that Crow and Sandy are the Westings.

She calls various heirs to the stand to establish that the game was orchestrated by Westing himself, disguised as Sandy. Turtle claims Westing was a sickly man, so he used the game as a way to say good-bye to family and friends before his actual death. After Turtle explains the case, Crow returns. The police had declared her innocent.

Only Turtle knows that Sam Westing is really still alive under yet another name, Julian R. Eastman, who poses as the chairman of Westing Corporation. Turtle deduces the final piece of the puzzle by observing that four names have a pattern: Sam Westing, Barney

Northrup, Sandy McSouthers, and finally Julian Eastman. They are all directions. Turtle wins the game, but she never tells any of the other heirs the final piece. She lets them go on thinking Julian Eastman is just the chairman, but she visits him often and grows very close to him.

Because only Turtle knows the real truth, some of the characters are upset that the game seems to have been an elaborate trick. However, other characters point out the things they have all gained from playing the game such as friendships, happiness, acceptance, and new, more fulfilling roles in life. The last three chapters jump ahead several years, showing how the characters' lives have progressed and improved even more since their involvement in the Westing Game.

5

THE READER AS A PLAYER

Often, mystery readers are able to gather pieces of information to solve the mystery, making them similar to a detective. Reader-response theory focuses on the reader's role in bringing meaning to the story through his or her own knowledge, experience, and opinions. *The Westing Game* provides bits of information the Westing heirs can piece together to form a complete picture. Raskin allows readers to play the game and fit the pieces of the puzzle together themselves rather than relying on a narrator. In *The Westing Game*, Raskin positions the reader as an active participant in the

THESIS

The thesis claims: "In *The Westing Game*, Raskin positions the reader as an active participant in the story through the literary devices of point of view, puns, and allusion." The author will examine how the reader is involved in the story by discussing three different literary devices.

Ray Walston played Sandy McSouthers in the 1997
The Westing Game television movie.

ARGUMENT ONE

The first argument explores the first literary device mentioned in the thesis, which is point of view: "The mystery bounces between diverse points of view, demanding reader attention and offering multiple options for connections between readers and characters." The author goes on to demonstrate that diverse points of view connect readers to the story and its characters.

story through the literary devices of point of view, puns, and allusion.

The mystery bounces between diverse points of view, demanding reader attention and offering multiple options for connections between readers and characters. **Point of view shifts come rapidly, sometimes between short** paragraphs and sometimes without clear tags to signal the change. This shifting is obvious in passages such as the following one between Chris and Mrs. Baumbach: "Mrs. Baumbach said her daughter might have been an artist if things had turned out differently. What would I have been if things had turned out differently?"[1] With no clear signal as to who is thinking, it is up to the reader to judge whether "I" is a shift back to Chris's point of view or to someone else's. Readers are responsible for tracking point of view. Because there is no single point of view until the end, when Turtle takes over as narrator, there is no dominant detective figure. Instead,

Raskin invites the reader to fill that role.

The novel also uses puns to encourage close reading and show readers words can be manipulated to create multiple meanings. At several points, the book draws attention to small puns. For example, characters are asked to fill out their positions on a legal form, which usually means they are to indicate their jobs. However, *position* can also refer to a person's posture or the location of a person's body. When filling out the form, Jake Wexler makes a joke on the double meaning, writing, "standing or sitting when not lying down."[2] Another example of this type of pun comes when Attorney Plum reads out the character pairings, including each character's name and position. Angela, who has no job, put "none" for her position. When the lawyer reads the position aloud, Angela's fiancé, Denton, wonders, "What in the world did Angela mean by 'nun'?"[3] In this line, the book plays on the identical pronunciations but very different meanings of *none* and *nun.* Small puns such as these encourage readers to pay close attention to words, considering both their obvious meanings and their hidden or multiple meanings.

The small puns also prepare readers for more complex word play in the book. The clues the pairs receive are an elaborate play on the song "America the Beautiful." Each of the pairs receives seemingly random words as clues, and they are told in the game instructions, "It's what you don't have that counts."[4] By paying close attention to the words, piecing them together into the song, and looking for what is missing, readers will be able to see that the missing words and letters spell out "Berthe Erica Crow." Characters in the novel eventually make the connection; however, readers have all the word clues necessary to come up with the answer before the book's characters do.

The object of the Westing Game is to come up with the answer, but another major mystery in the book has to do with who Sam Westing really is and what happened to him. The novel uses an overarching pun to leave clues for that mystery as well. This time, the word play draws on the directions of north, south, east, and west. Several characters in the novel have names including directions: Sam Westing, Julian R.

Eastman, Barney Northrup, and Sandy McSouthers. Those names are combined with the instructions, "The heir who wins the windfall will be the one who finds the . . . FOURTH."[5] The word play on the four directions from which the wind blows runs throughout the book and finally leads to the revelation that all four characters are aliases for and disguises of Sam "Windy" Windkloppel. By drawing attention to smaller puns, the novel encourages readers to be alert for running puns such as this one and to participate in creating the puns' meanings.

Finally, the novel uses national allusions young American readers are typically familiar with, which empowers them to draw on their knowledge to solve the mystery. Through the central character, Sam Westing, the book alludes to many national icons and ideals. He is presented as an Uncle Sam figure in his clothing and patriotism. As the son of immigrants turned successful business mogul, he also represents the American Dream. These icons

ARGUMENT THREE

The last argument focuses on the book's use of well-known allusions to encourages reader participation in the story: "Finally, the novel uses national allusions young American readers are typically familiar with, which empowers them to draw on their knowledge to solve the mystery."

and ideals, combined with the "America the Beautiful" song at the center of the clues, are frequently taught in US classrooms, so they appeal to readers' knowledge. By working off of readers' already established knowledge, the overt and accessible allusions encourage immediate participation.

Mysteries seem to be especially well suited for reader participation and reader-response theory because they usually revolve around an issue that needs to be resolved. *The Westing Game* uses literary devices such as point of view, puns, and allusions to create a story that gives readers the tools and room to participate in the story's resolution. As a result, this text prompts readers to consider the idea that they are just as important to a story as the author or the characters.

CONCLUSION

The essay ends with the conclusion, which reiterates the thesis and three arguments. The conclusion also draws a connection between reader participation and the mystery genre.

THINKING
CRITICALLY

Now it's your turn to assess the essay. Consider these questions:

1. Is there any evidence in the overview of *The Westing Game* that contradicts the essay's thesis?

2. Of the three literary devices covered in the essay, which do you think would be the most effective in drawing readers into the mystery?

3. *The Westing Game* was written in the 1970s. Are the book's national allusions, discussed in the essay's third argument, still relevant to contemporary readers, or are they outdated?

OTHER
APPROACHES

Reader-response theory is just one critical lens that can be used to explore the mystery genre in *The Westing Game*. Other essays could employ different critical lenses, such as Marxist theory or critical race theory.

Marxist Theory in *The Westing Game*

Marxist theory focuses on the dynamics between social classes and the ways wealth creates oppression in society. Many of the characters in *The Westing Game* are or have come from lower-class backgrounds, and they continue to struggle with the ties between money and identity. A thesis for this theory could be: Characters in the novel learn that financial motivation only leads to isolation; however, meaningful relationships with others and with oneself will lead to success of all kinds, including financial success.

Critical Race Theory in
The Westing Game

Critical race theory examines constructions of race and how certain racial groups are empowered or disempowered. *The Westing Game* has a diverse cast of characters whose backgrounds include many races, ethnicities, nationalities, abilities, ages, and religions. A thesis investigating the book through this lens could be: Sam Westing is a representative of many American ideals, including the concept of the melting pot, which says different races can mix harmoniously and contribute to the country's success.

6

OVERVIEWS OF SHERLOCK HOLMES WORKS

One of the best-known detectives in mystery fiction is Sherlock Holmes. Holmes's character first appeared in Sir Arthur Conan Doyle's 1887 *A Study in Scarlet*. Between 1901 and 1902, Doyle published *The Hound of the Baskervilles* as part of a series of stories about his famous detective Sherlock Holmes. Since then, many books, movies, and television shows have featured Holmes, evolving his character and developing new story lines for him. One example is Shane Peacock's *Eye of the Crow*, published in 2007, which tells the

Sir Arthur Conan Doyle wrote about Sherlock Holmes for 40 years.

story of what Sherlock Holmes was like as a teenager and how he became interested in solving crimes.

The Curse of the Baskervilles

The Hound of the Baskervilles begins in London, England, where Dr. James Mortimer seeks help from Sherlock Holmes in advising Henry Baskerville. Henry has suddenly become the heir of Baskerville Hall after the death of his uncle, Sir Charles. Mortimer then tells Holmes of the rumored curse of the Baskervilles, a tale involving a devilish hound that has preyed on the master of Baskerville Hall for generations. Sir Charles was deathly afraid of the hound, and indeed, when his body was found, the face was contorted in fear and footprints of a gigantic hound were close by. After considering Mortimer's evidence, Holmes reaches some preliminary theories. He believes Sir Charles had been waiting at the gate when he spotted someone or something that sent him running in fear. The exertion led to his death.

Meeting the New Heir

Henry arrives with Mortimer the next morning, bringing with him two mysterious pieces of information: a note warning Henry to stay away from Baskerville

Hall and news of a missing new boot. After hearing the details of his uncle's death, Henry requests some time to think. He asks Holmes and Dr. John Watson, Holmes's friend and sidekick, to join him for lunch later that day and leaves with Mortimer. Holmes and Watson follow them, observing that a bearded man in a cab is following as well.

Holmes and Watson arrive at Henry's hotel to find him upset over another missing boot, this time an old black one. Nevertheless, Henry says he intends to take up residence at Baskerville Hall, which is out on the moors near Dartmoor. Holmes suggests Watson accompany Henry for safety while Holmes stays in London to work on other cases.

Mysteries on the Moor

On the drive through the moors, Watson, Mortimer, and Henry see guards posted and learn that Selden, a notorious murderer, has escaped from prison. The party meets ominous circumstances at the hall as well. The Barrymores inform Henry that they will leave the household soon, and that night, Watson hears a woman crying. The next morning, Watson can see that Mrs. Barrymore had been crying, but Mr. Barrymore lies and says it wasn't her. More suspicion arises as Watson meets Stapleton, a neighbor and a naturalist. Miss Stapleton, his sister, mistakes Watson for Henry and secretly warns him to leave the moor and never return.

As Watson and Henry settle in, they learn more about the family curse. Stapleton takes them to the place where the hound killed his first victim, Sir Hugo, and Mortimer comes to the hall to walk Henry and Watson through the circumstances of Sir Charles's death. Meanwhile, more mysterious events occur at night. Watson sees Mr. Barrymore creeping through the hallways and looking out over the moor. Watson and Henry follow Mr. Barrymore and discover that he had been bringing food to the fugitive Selden, who is actually Mrs. Barrymore's brother. Mr. Barrymore begs Watson and Henry not to alert police. They agree because the Barrymores have arranged to send Selden to South America. In thanks, Mr. Barrymore offers information about Sir Charles's death that he had been withholding—Sir Charles had gone to the gate that night to meet a woman. Mr. Barrymore does not know the woman's name, only that her initials are L. L.

When Watson asks Mortimer about women with those initials, he reports that a neighbor of Baskerville Hall, Frankland, has a daughter, Laura Lyons.
Mrs. Lyons married a man who abandoned her, and several of the area residents including Mortimer, Sir Charles, and Stapleton had given her money to help her. Watson goes to see Mrs. Lyons. After much prodding, she admits she had written a letter to Sir Charles, requesting a meeting at the gate the night of his death in order to ask for financial assistance in obtaining a divorce. However, she never went because financial assistance came from another source.

Unraveling the Mysteries

After that errand, Watson goes in search of a strange man whom he and others have seen out on the moor. It turns out to be Holmes, who has been undercover to get a unique perspective on the case. Holmes then reveals several surprising details. The woman who has been posing as Stapleton's sister is actually his wife. She sent the warning in London, and Stapleton had been following Henry in the cab. Holmes also believes Stapleton to be the hound's keeper. Furthermore, though he is a married man, Stapleton has allowed

Mrs. Lyons to believe an engagement exists between them, which is why she sought a divorce. Holmes wants to meet with Mrs. Lyons the next day to enlist her as their ally.

As Watson and Holmes talk, they hear a man's screams and noises from the hound. They follow the sound to find a man fallen to his death. When they move to collect the body, they see it is Selden, dressed in Henry's old clothes, which Mr. Barrymore had given

Holmes and Watson know Stapleton had intended to kill Henry after finding Selden in Henry's clothes.

him. While they are with the body, Stapleton arrives, wondering if it is Henry.

Closing the Case

Holmes accompanies Watson back to Baskerville Hall. While perusing the family portraits, they notice a striking resemblance between Hugo Baskerville and Stapleton, thus deducing Stapleton is a Baskerville out for the inheritance. That establishes motive. The next day, Holmes instructs Henry to accept an invitation to the Stapletons' with a plan to catch Stapleton in the act. Meanwhile, Holmes and Watson go to speak with Mrs. Lyons. After learning Stapleton was using her, she tells them Stapleton instructed her to write the letter to Sir Charles. With that clue in place, Watson and Holmes meet Inspector Lestrade, who has arrived from London with a warrant.

The three take up their post, watching Stapleton and Henry. When Henry leaves, a huge, glowing hound barrels down on him. Holmes shoots it to death. The men inspect the creature and find it to be an unusual hybrid of hound and mastiff, bred for size and strength, and made to glow by applying a chemical preparation of phosphorous to its fur. They find Miss Stapleton tied

The hound appears to be a hybrid dog, created to terrify.

up inside the house, and she tells them her brother is probably hiding in an old mine out in the mire, where he kept the hound. Fog prevents them from traveling that night, but Miss Stapleton leads them there the next morning. They find Henry's old missing boot, used by Stapleton to give the hound his scent. They do not find Stapleton, but all evidence points to his drowning death in the mire.

An Overview of *Eye of the Crow*

In *Eye of the Crow*, young Sherlock Holmes, a 13-year-old, half-Jewish boy with no friends or sense of belonging, spends his days people-watching in London's Trafalgar

Square and reading discarded copies of *The Illustrated Police News*. In today's copy, he sees a drawing of a young woman lying dead, alongside the headline, "Murder!" When Sherlock returns to his family's shabby apartment, his father, Wilber, guesses he hasn't been at school. The two discuss Sherlock's day, and Sherlock is sure to mention the crows he saw, which interest Wilber because of his educational background studying birds. Before Wilber, the son of a poor Jewish immigrant, eloped with Sherlock's mother, Rose, the daughter of well-to-do Christian parents, he had planned to be a professor. However, he and Rose lost everything after their elopement because of societal disapproval of the mixed marriage. Now Wilber works as a humble bird trainer, and Rose gives music lessons to wealthy families. After discussing the Trafalgar Square crows with his father, Sherlock takes another look at the picture of the murdered woman and notices a crow overlooking the scene.

The next day, Sherlock reads that a young Arab, an immigrant from Egypt, named Mohammad Adalji has been arrested for the murder, and Sherlock goes to watch the police bring him to the courthouse. He is shocked by the rowdy mob and Mohammad's cries of innocence. Police suspect robbery as a motive because the woman's coin purse was missing. That evening, as Sherlock heads home, he detours, following the crows down the alley where the murder happened.

The next morning, Sherlock asks his father more about crows. Wilber tells him that researchers believe crows can communicate and that they are attracted to shiny things. Sherlock skips school again and returns to the murder scene. He realizes the crows seem to be looking for something and digging, so he does the same, turning up a glass eyeball. In the middle of the night, police come to the Holmes's door, asking why Sherlock had been at the murder scene two days in a row. They arrest him for possible involvement.

Undercover for Justice

Sherlock is placed in a jail cell next to Mohammad, who tells Sherlock his side of the story. If true, the story proves his innocence. A charitable man named Andrew C. Doyle and his daughter Irene come to see Mohammad. Irene returns to visit Sherlock several times, and she helps him escape. He flees to the Doyles' house, where Irene says she wants to be involved in solving the case. As their first step, they examine the

Eye of the Crow is set in London, with much of the plot's action taking place at Trafalgar Square.

eyeball, noting the iris is brown with violet flecks. They also see the letters *L* and *E* on it and guess those might be the manufacturer's initials.

Next, Sherlock examines the crime scene again. He notices how big the bloodstain is and decides it must have been a very violent crime, committed intentionally not randomly. He also observes the crows appear to be looking for something again, so he searches and finds an expensive bracelet. As he pockets the bracelet, he sees a man dressed in a black jacket with red slashes on it watching him.

Sherlock's next steps are to research glass-eye manufacturers and to interview neighbors. To do the first, he sends Irene to a library. To do the second, he asks Malefactor, the leader of a street gang, if his boys could ask around. Meanwhile, Sherlock picks up a newspaper to find out more about the victim. He discovers her name is Lillie Irving and that she was a young actress from a humble upbringing. Sherlock wonders why a minor actress would have such expensive jewelry, so he goes to the theater to investigate. He discovers Lillie knew a man who gave her diamonds and money.

The next day, Sherlock and Irene visit a glass-eye manufacturer with the initials found on the eye. They learn that the manufacturer makes products only for doctors in Mayfair, an upscale part of town. Sherlock is now getting a portrait of the suspect—a wealthy man, living in Mayfair, with one glass eye and one natural eye, both brown with violet specks. Next, Sherlock seeks out Malefactor to hear what he has learned. Based on the gang members' interviews, Malefactor reports a wealthy gentleman was seen fleeing the scene in a private coach,

Throughout the novel, Sherlock watches crows for signs to help solve the murder mystery.

black with red trimming. Sherlock knows he needs help from his mother, who gives music lessons in Mayfair.

He sneaks into his parents' flat, waking them and telling them everything. He asks his mother to observe the residents of Mayfair. Even though he warns her to be careful, Sherlock leaves feeling guilty for dragging his mother into danger. When he returns to the Doyles', he finds a dead crow pinned up along with the warning "Beware Jew!" written in blood. He cleans up the scene and wanders into the night.

Sacrificing for Justice

Sherlock returns the next day to tell Irene she can no longer be involved in the dangerous mystery. Irene does not heed his warning. Instead, she follows him, and the black coach with red trim runs over her. Irene survives the attack, and Sherlock sneaks into her hospital room to tell her again not to be involved. Though it is painful, he is willing to give up friendship for the sake of justice.

Two days later, Sherlock meets his mother on the street to find out if she has any information. She does not, so Sherlock asks her to be braver and make direct inquiries. In the meantime, Sherlock sharpens his skills of observation and living covertly on the street. He is even able to eavesdrop on a conversation between Malefactor and Irene, in which Irene says she observed the black coach near the Holmes's flat. Fearing danger, Sherlock goes immediately to meet his mother. She has found the names and addresses of four men with glass eyes.

Sherlock disguises himself as a chimney sweep to enter the Mayfair homes secretly and search them. He rules out the three homes, but before he searches the last house, he feels very strongly that he needs to see his mother, so he returns to their flat. His mother arrives late, acting strangely. Her job that day had been at the home of the fourth suspect. She knew that but went anyway to help Sherlock. A gentleman at the home served her poisoned tea, and she dies in front of Sherlock.

Filled with rage, Sherlock steals a knife. He runs to the fourth house, planning revenge. Once there, Sherlock searches for the hard proof he needs. He finds Lillie's coin purse with a note inside. The note explains that Lillie and the man were having an affair, that Lillie was threatening to blackmail him, and that they had arranged one final meeting—at the place where she was found dead. Sherlock reaches for his stolen knife and prepares to kill the man. However, he stops himself. He knows murder would not be justice. He would rather turn over the man to the authorities, so he gathers one more piece of evidence: he slaps the man across the face to see the color of his eyes—brown with violet flecks.

In disguise, Holmes delivers the bracelet, glass eye, purse, letter, and a detailed explanation of the crime and perpetrator to the police. The explanation also mentions his mother's bravery and sacrifice. Mohammad is set free and the real murderer is arrested, but Sherlock is disappointed to see that the newspaper story makes no mention of his mother. He vows to close himself off emotionally and devote his life to seeking justice.

UNDERSTANDING SHERLOCK HOLMES

A common feature in mystery literature is a detective character who makes sense of the crime and brings resolution. Some literary critics who study the structure of mysteries argue these detectives are part of a predictable formula used in mystery fiction not only to solve the story's mystery but also to explain away the scary situations and cultural fears underlying the mystery. An essay looking at how mysteries use Sherlock Holmes as a formulaic character to explain uncertainty and fear would consider patterns in the detective's personality, behavior, and methods across various books.

There are many differences in the ways Doyle and Peacock present Sherlock Holmes in their works.

Sherlock Holmes's character is an example of a predictable, formulaic detective.

For example, Doyle's Holmes is a confident and successful expert, but Peacock's Holmes is a loner from a poor family. Despite these differences, each book uses the character to explore major social issues. Doyle's story examines worries about scientific advancement in Victorian England. Peacock's novel examines the fear of outsiders, which was a problem in Victorian England as well as a problem that continues to plague many countries in the early twenty-first century, when Peacock wrote his novel.

In both *The Hound of the Baskervilles* and *Eye of the Crow*, the authors use the character of Sherlock Holmes to dispel prevalent cultural fears.

Both Doyle and Peacock build their mysteries around serious cultural fears. At the time when *The Hound of the Baskervilles* is set, science was presenting new technological possibilities

THESIS STATEMENT

At the end of the introduction, the thesis asserts: "In both *The Hound of the Baskervilles* and *Eye of the Crow*, the authors use the character of Sherlock Holmes to dispel prevalent cultural fears." This essay will explore the cultural fears present in the two books and how each Sherlock Holmes character shows there is really nothing to fear.

ARGUMENT ONE

First, the author explains the cultural fears present in each book: "Both Doyle and Peacock build their mysteries around serious cultural fears." Doyle works with the Victorian fear of science, while Peacock engages the fear of ethnic, national, religious, and economic outsiders.

and offering worldly explanations for things previously explained by religion. As a result, some people worried science could lead to unnatural and evil creations.

The figure at the center of the Baskerville legend, the hound, represents the fear of those evil and supernatural creations. According to that legend, the dog is a "hound of hell," a huge beast with a taste for blood.[1] Characters describe the animal as "spectral" and "monstrous."[2] Those descriptions portray the hound as a demon from a fantasy story rather than something with a logical explanation.

Later in the novel, readers find out the hound does have an explanation. It turns out the hound used by the murderous Stapleton is actually a scientific creation instead of a normal, natural dog. Rather than being a pure hound, the dog is a hybrid of mastiff and bloodhound, set aglow with a "cunning preparation" of phosphorous by Stapleton, who is a kind of scientist.[3] Therefore, the hound demonstrates the fear of unnatural science coming to life. Stapleton draws on that fear to commit his crimes.

Whereas Doyle's novel works with cultural fears of science and the unnatural, Peacock's works with fears of ethnic, national, religious, and economic outsiders who were seen as threats to the upper-class way of life in Victorian England. Sherlock's father, Wilber, is Jewish and the son of an Eastern European immigrant. When Wilber fell in love with Sherlock's mother, Rose, a Christian woman from a wealthy English family, society disapproved of the couple, so they eloped. There were severe consequences to their marriage. Rose's parents disowned her, and Wilber lost his promising career at the university. They are forced to work in humble service jobs and live in a shabby flat. In his status as a poor, half-Jewish boy, Sherlock is a minority, who is seen as an outsider, threatening the status quo. In expressions of hatred and fear, others label Sherlock as "'alf-breed Jew boy."[4]

Another major character in the book, the accused murderer, Mohammad Adalji, is an outsider as well. Mohammad is originally from Egypt, and he is a practicing Muslim. Because Mohammad is an outsider, he is an ideal person to blame for the crime. People are eager to pin the murder on "a street person, a foreigner."[5] When authorities find him covered in blood with the murder weapon on hand, they quickly arrest him for the crime without performing a thorough investigation. Similar to Sherlock, Mohammad is the victim of slurs and prejudices. For example, his jailers refuse to tell him which direction east is, which is a requirement for saying his prayers properly.

In both works, Holmes's character embodies reason, a quality that allows him to counter fear. In Doyle's novel, Holmes takes a rational approach to the legend and the hound. At the beginning and end of the book, Holmes walks readers through the process of uncovering mysteries by observing facts. Holmes applies those methods immediately when Dr. Mortimer comes to discuss Sir Charles's death. Rather than believing the "fairy tales" of the supernatural hound, Holmes asks for the facts and undermines the fantastical aspects of the case.[6] For instance, he tells Dr. Mortimer, "You must admit that the footmark is material."[7] Holmes displays the same grounded, practical mindset later in the novel when he encounters the hound. He is not overcome by fearful emotion when the hound tries to attack Sir Henry. He does not buy into the myth that the hound

ARGUMENT TWO

Next, the author lays out the qualities within the Holmes characters that explain away cultural fear: "In both works, Holmes's character embodies reason, a quality that allows him to counter fear."

is a larger-than-life monster, impossible to kill. Instead, Holmes chases down the hound and shoots it to death.

Similar to Doyle's Holmes, Peacock's Holmes demonstrates interest in facts and reason to explain what others fear. Whereas other characters are quick to condemn both Sherlock and Mohammad because they are outsiders, Sherlock favors factual evidence over stereotyping and profiling. To prove Mohammad is innocent, Sherlock gathers clues meticulously. He observes the crows at the crime scene, researches the glass eyeballs, and investigates suspects' addresses. He is swayed by evidence, not empathy for or prejudice against the accused Mohammad.

Similar to the older Holmes in Doyle's novel, the teenage Sherlock in Peacock's is able to choose an intellectual mindset instead of an emotional one. When Sherlock finds the true murderer, who has also killed his mother, he resists violence and revenge, choosing justice instead. That choice shows Sherlock is different from those who give into fear and anger.

Both Holmes characters conquer fear by turning the threats on their heads. In *The Hound of the Baskervilles*, Holmes uses the explanatory power of science, referring to his investigative methods as "scientific use of the imagination" to solve crime.[8] Doyle's Holmes is a gentleman, a well-respected member of the community, and a man of superior intellect. By channeling science through a proper English gentleman, the book makes science seem normal,

ARGUMENT THREE

In the final argument, the author claims: "Both Holmes characters conquer fear by turning the threats on their heads." The paragraphs in this argument show how the Holmes characters use what had been feared in order to solve crime, which makes that thing seem positive rather than scary.

even upper class and something to be admired, rather than threatening. At the same time, the story does not ignore science can be misused to create evil, which Stapleton does in constructing his hound. However, the story emphasizes such evil is the product of bad men, not science. Good men, on the other hand, should not fear science. Instead, good men can use science to explain the things people fear.

In a similar way, *Eye of the Crow* turns the perceived social threat of outsiders around. In Peacock's story, the outsider is the victor, not the villain. The poor, half-Jewish Sherlock defeats evil and exposes crime. Furthermore, he proves that another outsider, the Muslim immigrant Mohammad, is innocent. Instead, the murderer is an upper-class British man. In this interesting turn, the book suggests people should not fear ethnic and religious outsiders as the source of crime and evil. Rather, they should consider that sources of evil may come from privileged and powerful members of society.

Neither *The Hound of the Baskervilles* nor *Eye of the Crow* is a simple story of crime and detection. Although investigation of murder is certainly a major focus in each book, the novels are also interested in investigating deeper cultural issues and social fears through the detective character Sherlock Holmes. In both novels, the Sherlock Holmes figures are able to chase away illogical social fears and demonstrate how the things people fear can actually be assets.

CONCLUSION

The conclusion reemphasizes the introduction's thesis and the body paragraphs' arguments. In addition, the conclusion links the essays back to broad ideas about the mystery genre.

THINKING
CRITICALLY

Now it is your turn to assess the essay. Consider these questions:

1. Is the author's thesis credible and supported?

2. Does the author balance examination of the two novels fairly?

3. Peacock's novel is set in the mid-nineteenth century, but it
    was written in the early twenty-first century. Do the prejudices
    and fears presented in his book reflect the period in which
    the novel was written, the period in which it was set, or both?
    Do the cultural fears present in Doyle's early twentieth-century
    book have any relevance today?

OTHER

APPROACHES

The previous essay is only one example of how to analyze the detective in mystery novels, by examining the character's role as a reassuring figure who can dispel cultural fears. An alternate approach to the Sherlock Holmes novels may study the significance of setting in the novels. Another approach could investigate the type of heroism displayed in Sherlock Holmes characters.

Setting in Detective Novels

There is a very strong sense of setting in both *The Hound of the Baskervilles* and *Eye of the Crow*. *The Hound of the Baskervilles* emphasizes the wilderness of the moors, whereas *Eye of the Crow* presents many different parts of London, including its busy public squares, impoverished sectors, and affluent neighborhoods. A thesis for an approach focusing on setting could be: Both Doyle and Peacock use strong, chaotic settings to highlight Sherlock Holmes's ability to control chaos through intellectual power.

The Heroism of Sherlock Holmes

Sherlock Holmes is the hero of *Eye of the Crow*. However, he is not an epic hero nor is he an action hero. Instead, he is an intellectual hero. An essay exploring the type of heroism constructed in Sherlock Holmes could compare his mental capabilities to his physical capabilities. A thesis for this approach could be: The character of Sherlock Holmes presents intellectual heroism as an alternate to traditional concepts of physical heroism.

8

AN OVERVIEW OF
A SPY IN THE HOUSE

A Spy in the House, the first book in Y. S. Lee's Agency series, was published in 2009. The novel is a young adult historical mystery featuring a strong female protagonist.

Joining the Agency

Twelve-year-old orphan Mary Lang is sentenced to death for housebreaking, but as she is led from court, she is chloroformed and taken to Miss Scrimshaw's Academy for Girls, a school designed to give girls an education and independent life. This is an unusual proposition for women in London in the middle of the nineteenth century.

In 2011, Lee's *A Spy in the House* won the Canadian Children's Book Centre's John Spray Mystery Award.

Five years later, Mary requests a meeting with
the school's head teachers, Miss Anne Treleaven and
Mrs. Felicity Frame, to discuss her future. By that time,
Mary has become an assistant teacher at the school, but
she wants a more satisfying career. The head teachers
introduce Mary to the Agency, an organization of
intelligent women who leverage women's domestic roles
to gather sensitive information for clients and solve
mysteries. Mary's first assignment is to investigate a
merchant named Henry Thorold. Thorold is suspected
of smuggling stolen artifacts from India. Mary infiltrates
Thorold's home by serving as a companion to his
daughter, Angelica.

On Mary's first Saturday there, the Thorolds host
a party. Mary takes the opportunity to slip away and
search Thorold's office, but she does not find anything
useful. Before she can leave, she hears footsteps
approaching, so she hides in the wardrobe. Someone
else is already hiding there. A man cups his hand over
her mouth and instructs her to remain quiet until the
servant who has entered the room leaves. The man is
19-year-old James Easton.

James begins investigating Mary. He and ten-year-old
Alfred Quigley, whom he has employed as a tracker

The Agency believes Thorold is selling smuggled Indian artifacts in London and Paris, France.

and spy, follow her when she sneaks into Thorold's warehouse to search files. As she leaves, James catches her, forces her into his carriage, and suggests the two share information. James explains he has been investigating unsavory business rumors against Thorold: that he has been claiming to lose cargo in shipwrecks when really he sells the cargo himself and pockets the profits. James cares about the allegations because his brother George wants to marry Angelica. When it is Mary's turn to share her reason for being at the warehouse, she lies and says she is researching one of Thorold's former maids. James recommends they collaborate. Mary finally agrees after another of her break-in attempts is unsuccessful.

Life as a Double Agent

Mary begins finding out mysterious things about the Thorolds. Mrs. Thorold's coachman says she claims to go to the doctor every day, but really she is having an affair or conducting some other secret activity. Mary also catches Thorold's secretary Michael Gray and Angelica engaged in secret conversations and meetings. Meanwhile, James has discovered that Thorold has made financial arrangements with the Lascars, a charity for old and impoverished Asian sailors. He wonders if Thorold may be using the charity as a place to hide information or smuggled goods.

They find neither at the charity, but Mary does discover secrets about her past. The warden, Mr. Chen, talks with Mary about her father, who was a Chinese sailor. He also gives Mary a box her father left before his death. Inside is a note, a jade pendant, and other papers. Gray also arrives at the Lascars while Mary is inside. Later that night, Mary overhears Gray tell Thorold that he went to look into a large donation from Thorold's business accounts. Thorold tells Gray not to inquire further.

The next day, Mary follows Gray and Angelica to a church, where Mary observes another secret: she witnesses the couple getting married. After the brief ceremony, Mary asks about their future, and Gray says they will keep the marriage secret while he looks for other employment. He wants to leave his position with Thorold because he finds some of the company's large payments and accounting activity suspicious.

Mary finds the questionable financial documents Gray has hidden and takes them to James. The documents show Thorold has made frequent insurance claims and that the insurance company has opened an investigation for insurance fraud. The investigation has been assigned to a man named Joseph Mays, whom Thorold appears to be bribing. After they finish going through the documents, Mary and James notice Mrs. Thorold driving through an unusual part of town. They follow and watch her walk into a house she has been renting under a fake name, but they find no evidence linking her to Thorold's illegal businesses practices.

A jade pendant was one of the belongings left behind for Mary by her father.

Concluding the First Assignment

The next day, several developments occur. Quigley is found dead at the Eastons' construction site. Police believe it to be an accident, but James suspects Thorold. Meanwhile, police arrest Thorold for smuggling goods after raiding one of his ships. Mary delivers the news to James, who tells her to stop her investigation because he fears for her safety. He does not explain his reasons to Mary well, so she leaves their partnership angry.

Back at the Thorolds, Mrs. Thorold has discovered Angelica and Gray's marriage. She fires Mary, says Gray will be arrested, and throws Angelica out without a penny. Angelica then reveals she plans to have her marriage to Gray annulled and that she will move to Vienna, Austria, which is something she had discussed that morning with Mary.

Meanwhile, James reads one last note from Quigley, which indicates he has uncovered some information at the Lascars' refuge. James goes over to the charity house to search for the information, where Mrs. Thorold attacks him. She is mad that James had been using Quigley to spy on her covert business locations. It is true that Thorold had been smuggling artifacts and making false insurance claims; however, Mrs. Thorold is even worse. She has been using pirates to steal goods from her husband's ships. She killed Quigley and Mr. Chen, and she plans to kill James as well. She knocks him out and sets fire to the charity. Mary is able to get to there just in time to save James.

In a debriefing with the Agency, Mary reviews the case with Anne and Felicity. They confirm Thorold had been smuggling goods, making false insurance claims, bribing Mays during the insurance investigation, and using cheap foreign labor to make as much profit as possible. Meanwhile, unbeknownst to Thorold, his wife had been using pirates to attack his ships. At the time of the debriefing, Mrs. Thorold remained at large.

Mary returns to the burnt-down Lascars house hoping to find the box with her father's papers still intact, but workers there tell her everything has been destroyed. James is there, too, paying respects to Mr. Chen. James and Mary discuss why Mrs. Thorold killed him. Mary's theory is that Mr. Chen had begun to suspect her because some of the Lascars working on the ships may have found out she was behind the pirate attacks. James tells Mary he is going to Calcutta to oversee his company's railroad construction. The two part amicably.

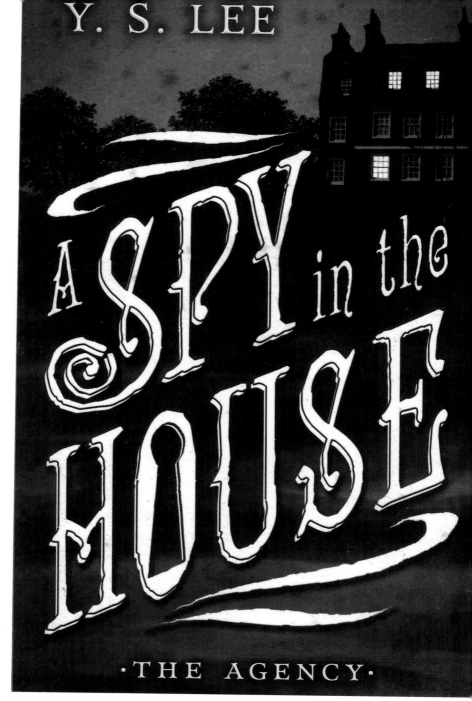

Y. S. LEE

A SPY in the HOUSE

· THE AGENCY ·

A Spy in the House was a finalist for the Agatha Award in the best children's and young adult category.

9

WOMEN'S HISTORY AND MYSTERY

One of the major subgenres of mystery fiction is the historical mystery. Within this subgenre, some fiction makes use of real events from the past. Other fiction uses history more as a setting and a backdrop without working too closely with real events, which is the case in Y. S. Lee's *A Spy in the House*. Both types allow authors and readers to explore traditions, expectations, and norms of the past such as those surrounding gender roles. The mystery format also encourages authors and readers to treat gender concepts from the past as mysteries

A Spy in the House is set in London during the Victorian era.

themselves, which deserve questioning and investigation. A critical feminist approach to *A Spy in the House* could explore how the novel critiques historical constructions of women.

A Spy in the House is a historical mystery written in the twenty-first century but focused on the lives of strong female characters from the past. The main character, 17-year-old Mary Lang, works as a double agent in Victorian London, a period when women were traditionally viewed as more passive, weak, and limited than their male counterparts. However, this novel challenges those traditions with skilled, active, and ambitious female figures, including Mary, her instructors at the Agency, and the story's villainess. The historical mystery format of *A Spy in the House* allows the book to investigate gender stereotypes of the past and critique conventional roles of women from a twenty-first-century perspective.

THESIS STATEMENT

The author's thesis explains: "The historical mystery format of *A Spy in the House* allows the book to investigate gender stereotypes of the past and critique conventional roles of women from a twenty-first-century perspective." The essay discusses traditional concepts of women's roles and how this novel challenges those concepts.

Female characters in the novel hold positions traditionally considered masculine in the nineteenth century. **Mary works as an operative for the Agency, posing as a domestic companion for Angelica Thorold while really spying** on her father's business affairs. The Agency gives women challenging and intellectually stimulating alternatives to the few traditional professions open to them in the mid-nineteenth century. Rather than focusing solely on raising children, cleaning, or cooking, women working for the Agency can involve themselves in the masculine realms of crime, detection, business, and information. In addition to the women working within the Agency, the novel also features female characters in other conventionally masculine roles. Mrs. Thorold, for instance, takes on the role of villain by directing a crew of pirates.

Female characters in the novel pair their masculine roles with their femininity, and this combination often makes them more successful or gives them more

ARGUMENT ONE

The author first points out that characters in the book challenge gender perceptions by assuming roles that were considered more masculine than feminine at the times when the book is set: "Female characters in the novel hold positions traditionally considered masculine in the nineteenth century."

capabilities than male characters. In *A Spy in the House*, the women who train Mary at the Agency explain, "We place our agents in very sensitive situations. But while a man in such a position might be subject to suspicion, we find that women—posing as governesses or domestic servants, for example—are often totally ignored."[1] The Agency instructors suggest smart women can use these supposedly menial positions to their advantage in ways men would never suspect. They also add that their female operatives are "more perceptive," "less arrogant," "less prone to error," and "contrary to stereotype . . . often more logical" than men would be.[2]

Throughout the novel, female characters do, in fact, demonstrate more success and more cunning than male characters by using traditionally female positions to their advantages. For instance, Mary pieces together elements of the case that have escaped her male counterpart, James Easton, who is also investigating Mr. Thorold.

At the end of the novel, James asks, "I hoped you could explain something to me. . . . How did Mr. Chen fit into all of this?"[3] Mary knows the answer because of her background, and the wording shows James relies on Mary for information he cannot locate or comprehend himself. In another example, Mrs. Thorold, who exploits the perception of feminine weakness and poses as an invalid, proves herself smarter and more villainous than her husband. She is the mastermind behind the theft and piracy that undermines her husband's business.

Finally, the novel presents its female characters with other options beside marriage, which was often considered the only path for women in the nineteenth century. *A Spy in the House* allows young female characters to explore career options instead of restricting them to domestic relationships. When Mary first becomes a secret agent, she does so because she wants "satisfaction" from her work.[4] Even when she

ARGUMENT THREE

In the third argument, the author observes that the novel presents female characters with futures beyond the traditionally perceived path of marriage: "Finally, the novel presents its female characters with other options beside marriage, which was often considered the only path for women in the nineteenth century."

does become interested in James, she does not want him to "court her or anything ridiculous like that."[5] Mary realizes that would be silly because both she and James are too young for marriage and because she wants to continue her work with the Agency. Angelica also chooses to pursue her education and a career as a musician instead of marry.

Mysteries offer a perfect opportunity to ask questions and challenge assumptions, and historical mysteries in particular provide the chance to question assumptions from the past. *A Spy in the House* places strong, active female characters at the center of the mystery to critique the stereotypical ways women were perceived in the nineteenth century. Some of the novel's scenarios would not have been realistic options for nineteenth-century women; however, the novel lays out those scenarios to show alternatives that would have been more liberating than the limited gender roles that did exist.

CONCLUSION

The conclusion repeats the thesis for emphasis and ties the thesis back to the historical mystery subgenre.

THINKING
CRITICALLY

Now it is your turn to assess the essay. Consider these questions:

1. Do you agree with the essay's thesis? Is there evidence that disproves the thesis?

2. What is another argument you could add to support the author's thesis?

3. The author focuses on gender roles as they relate to female characters. Does the novel challenge historical perceptions of masculine identity as well?

OTHER
APPROACHES

The gender studies approach is just one of many critiques that can be applied to this historical mystery, as well as many other texts. Another approach to *A Spy in the House* might discuss national identity rather than gender identity. Yet another might explore the construction of villains.

National Identity in *A Spy in the House*

National identity sets the main character apart from others in *A Spy in the House*. Mary is a half-Chinese, half-Irish teenager living in London, though she does her best to hide her Chinese ancestry. A thesis exploring national identity in this historical mystery could be: Uncovering identity is often an important feature of historical mysteries, and Lee's novel emphasizes that national heritage affects identity whether a character wants it to or not.

Creating Villains in Historical Novels

Not all mysteries have villains, but many do. In *A Spy in the House*, the villain is Mrs. Thorold. Women at the Agency speculate Mrs. Thorold's evil actions are motivated by revenge against an unfair husband or the desire to overcome inferiority. A thesis exploring the villainous character could be: The novel suggests evil is complex and that enemies are never entirely, purely bad.

ANALYZE IT!

Now that you have learned different approaches to analyzing a work, are you ready to perform your own analysis? You have read that this type of evaluation can help you look at literature in a new way and make you pay attention to certain issues you may not have otherwise recognized. So, why not use one of these approaches to consider a fresh take on your favorite work?

First, choose a philosophy, critical theory, or other approach and consider which work or works you want to analyze. Remember the approach you choose is a springboard for asking questions about the works.

Next, write a specific question that relates to your approach or philosophy. Then you can form your thesis, which should provide the answer to that question. Your thesis is the most important part of your analysis and offers an argument about the work, considering its characters, plot, or literary techniques, or what it says about society or the world. Recall that the thesis statement typically appears at the very end of the introductory paragraph of your essay. It is usually only one sentence long.

After you have written your thesis, find evidence to back it up. Good places to start are in the work itself or in journals or articles that discuss what other people have said about it. You may also want to read about the author or creator's life so you can get a sense of what factors may have affected the creative process. This can be especially useful if you are considering how the work connects to history or the author's intent.

You should also explore parts of the book that seem to disprove your thesis and create an argument against them. As you do this, you might want to address what others have written about the book. Their quotes may help support your claim.

Before you start analyzing a work, think about the different arguments made in this book. Reflect on how evidence supporting the thesis was presented. Did you find that some of the techniques used to back up the arguments were more convincing than others? Try these methods as you prove your thesis in your own analysis paper.

When you are finished writing your analysis, read it over carefully. Is your thesis statement understandable? Do the supporting arguments flow logically, with the topic of each paragraph clearly stated? Can you add any information that would present your readers with a stronger argument in favor of your thesis? Were you able to use quotes from the book, as well as from other critics, to enhance your ideas?

Did you see the work in a new light?

GLOSSARY

DEBRIEFING
A meeting after a completed mission or assignment in which questions are answered and information is exchanged.

ELOPE
To marry in secret.

FORMULAIC
Following an established pattern or set of rules.

INSURANCE FRAUD
A harmful act committed on purpose to a person, place, or thing in order to collect money from an insurance policy.

PUN

A joke built on the different meanings a word can have.

RED HERRING

Something used to distract attention from the real issue.

RUSE

An action intended to trick or deceive.

SUBGENRE

A smaller category within a particular type of literature, art, music, or film.

ADDITIONAL
RESOURCES

SELECTED BIBLIOGRAPHY

Christie, Agatha. *The Murder of Roger Ackroyd*. 1926. New York: William Morrow, 2011. Print.

Doyle, Arthur Conan. *The Hound of the Baskervilles*. 1901–1902. New York: Modern Library, 2002. Print.

Faktorovich, Anna. *The Formulas of Popular Fiction: Elements of Fantasy, Science Fiction, Romance, Religious and Mystery Novels.* Jefferson, NC: McFarland, 2014. Print.

Lee, Y. S. *A Spy in the House*. Somerville, MA: Candlewick, 2009. Print.

Malmgren, Carl D. *Anatomy of a Murder: Mystery, Detective, and Crime Fiction*. Bowling Green, OH: Bowling Green State UP, 2001. Print.

Peacock, Shane. *Eye of the Crow*. Toronto: Tundra, 2007. Print.

Raskin, Ellen. *The Westing Game*. New York: Avon, 1978. Print.

Sussex, Lucy. *Women Writers and Detectives in Nineteenth-Century Crime Fiction: The Mothers of the Mystery Genre*. New York: Palgrave Macmillan, 2010. Print.

FURTHER READINGS

Brunsdale, Mitzi. *Icons of Mystery and Crime Detection: From Sleuths to Superheroes*. 2 vols. Santa Barbara, CA: Greenwood, 2010. Print.

Cortez, Sarah, ed. *You Don't Have a Clue: Latino Mystery Stories for Teens*. Houston, TX: Piñata Books, 2011. Print.

WEBSITES

To learn more about Essential Literary Genres, visit **booklinks.abdopublishing.com**. These links are routinely monitored and updated to provide the most current information available.

FOR MORE INFORMATION

Mystery Writers of America
1140 Broadway, Suite 1507, New York, NY 10001
212-888-8171
http://mysterywriters.org/
Mystery Writers of America is a literary society for authors that also provides information to the general public. The organization is responsible for administering the Edgar Awards every year to honor the best mystery literature.

The Sherlock Holmes Society of London
41 Sandford Road, Chelmsford CM2 6DE, United Kingdom
44-1245-284006
http://www.sherlock-holmes.org.uk/
This society is dedicated to the world of Sherlock Holmes. The society puts forth a scholarly journal while also organizing social events.

Sisters in Crime
PO Box 442124, Lawrence, KS 66044
758-842-1325
http://www.sistersincrime.org/
This organization connects authors and book professionals who are interested in women's mystery writing. The organization is also a source of information for anyone who would like to know more about women's contributions to the mystery genre.

SOURCE NOTES

CHAPTER 1. INTRODUCTION TO LITERARY GENRES
None.

CHAPTER 2. AN OVERVIEW OF *THE MURDER OF ROGER ACKROYD*
None.

CHAPTER 3. THE UNRELIABLE NARRATOR

1. Agatha Christie. *The Murder of Roger Ackroyd*. 1926. New York: William Morrow, 2011. Print. 147.

2. Ibid. 6.

3. Ibid. 243.

4. Ibid. 160.

CHAPTER 4. AN OVERVIEW OF *THE WESTING GAME*

1. Ellen Raskin. *The Westing Game*. New York: Avon, 1978. Print. 114.

CHAPTER 5. THE READER AS A PLAYER

1. Ellen Raskin. *The Westing Game*. New York: Avon, 1978. Print. 112.

2. Ibid. 33.

3. Ibid. 35.

4. Ibid. 36.

5. Ibid.

CHAPTER 6. OVERVIEWS OF SHERLOCK HOLMES WORKS

None.

CHAPTER 7. UNDERSTANDING SHERLOCK HOLMES

1. Arthur Conan Doyle. *The Hound of the Baskervilles*. 1901–1902. New York: Modern Library, 2002. Print. 13.

2. Ibid. 80.

3. Ibid. 153.

4. Shane Peacock. *The Eye of the Crow*. Toronto: Tundra, 2007. Print. 5.

5. Ibid. 4.

6. Arthur Conan Doyle. *The Hound of the Baskervilles*. 1901–1902. New York: Modern Library, 2002. Print. 14.

7. Ibid. 34.

8. Ibid.

CHAPTER 8. AN OVERVIEW OF *A SPY IN THE HOUSE*

None.

CHAPTER 9. WOMEN'S HISTORY AND MYSTERY

1. Y. S. Lee. *A Spy in the House*. Somerville, MA: Candlewick, 2009. Print. 20.

2. Ibid. 20.

3. Ibid. 331.

4. Ibid. 12.

5. Ibid. 327.

INDEX

ABOUT THE AUTHOR

Rebecca Morris has a PhD in English from Texas A&M University. She is coeditor of *Representing Children in Chinese and US Children's Literature* (Ashgate, 2014) and a contributor to *Jacqueline Wilson* (ed. Lucy Pearson, Palgrave Macmillan New Casebooks, 2015). Morris has also written literary guides for educational websites.